Hear ye! Hear ye! Noble Vikings beware.

Hägar the Horrible, that fearless but lovable Viking, is at it again. This time Hägar, his family and his sidekick Lucky Eddie are setting sail in a new giant size edition full of madcap fun and adventures!

HÄGAR
the Horrible

OL' BLUE EYES IS BACK!

by

Dik Browne

A Tempo Star Book

Distributed by Ace Books
Grosset & Dunlap, Inc., Publishers
New York, N.Y. 10010
A Filmways Company

HAGAR THE HORRIBLE—OL' BLUE EYES IS BACK!

ISBN: 0-441-31586-0

Tempo Books is registered in the U.S. Patent Office

Published simultaneously in Canada
Printed in the United States of America

HOW DO YOU LIKE MY COAT OF ARMS?
NICE, BUT WHAT DOES IT SAY?
DIK BROWNE 5-13

"I GOT MINE"
UBI BENE IBI PATRIA

LOOK, HELGA! I CAN TOUCH MY TOES!
DIK BROWNE 5-9
©1979 King Features Syndicate, Inc. World rights reserved.

WONDERFUL! WHILE YOU'RE DOWN THERE PICK UP YOUR MESS!!

LUCKY EDDIE JUST GOT HIS BIG BREAK!
GREAT!
3-16
DIK BROWNE

I KNEW HIS LUCK WOULD CHANGE!

OH...
©1979 King Features Syndicate, Inc. World rights reserved.

©1979 King Features Syndicate, Inc. World rights reserved.
GOOD BOY, SNERT!

DIK BROWNE 3-15

NOW *THAT'S* WHAT I CALL A HUNTING DOG!

NOW, LISTEN! I DON'T WANT THIS GOING IN ONE EAR AND OUT THE OTHER!
5-7
DIK BROWNE

OKAY! I'M READY!

THERE'S MORE TO BEING A VIKING THAN SAILING A BIG BOAT, INVADING ENGLAND AND STORMING CASTLES

THERE ARE THE DULL DAY-TO-DAY THINGS THAT HAVE TO BE DONE...
SLAYING DRAGONS...
RESCUING MAIDENS...
5-12
DIK BROWNE

MEN DON'T LIKE WOMEN WHO ARE TOO SMART. THEY LIKE WOMEN WHO SEEM TO BE DUMBER THAN THEY ARE!

DUMBER THAN THEY ARE?!! **HOW** DO YOU DO THAT?!
5-31
DIK BROWNE

YOU GOT TO BE VERY SMART.

I HAVE A TOUCHY STOMACH. IS THAT EASY TO DIGEST ?

IT'S PICKLED ALLIGATOR SKIN WITH HARD SAUCE

THAT SHOULD BE OKAY.
4-10 DIK BROWNE

HALF THE PEOPLE IN THIS WORLD ARE SELFISH, DIRTY AND IGNORANT!
WHAT'S THE OTHER HALF ?
DIK BROWNE 4-11

WOMEN.
©1979 King Features Syndicate, Inc. World rights reserved.

DOES IT HURT ?
HERE AND THERE
© 1979 King Features Syndicate, Inc. World rights reserved.

ARE YOU DIZZY ?
NOW AND THEN

FEEL NAUSEOUS ?
OFF AND ON...

DIK BROWNE 5-10
IS IT SERIOUS ?
YES AND NO

THEY'RE NOT MAKING KNIGHTS LIKE THEY USED TO!
©1979 King Features Syndicate, Inc. World rights reserved.

OR DRAGONS EITHER
DIK BROWNE -5-17

WHAT'S THAT ?!
HOT LEMONADE

C'MON, LUCKY EDDIE!

I'LL TRY ONE LAST SHOT

DIK BROWNE 4-12

I HAVEN'T WHISTLED AT A GIRL IN YEARS. BET I STILL CAN!

SIGH
SAME RESULTS!
DIK BROWNE 6-20

CAN I HELP YOU PACK ?
NAW, I'M NOT TAKING THAT MUCH...
DIK BROWNE 5-26
©1979 King Features Syndicate, Inc. World rights reserved.

IT'S JUST A BUSINESS TRIP

HAGAR INSULTED ME YESTERDAY AND I'M HERE TO MAKE HIM APOLOGIZE!
HE WAS IN AN AWFUL MOOD YESTERDAY
DIK BROWNE
5-25

TAKE A NUMBER

CONGRATULATIONS! WE VIKINGS HAVE JUST DISCOVERED THE NIAGARA RIVER!!
'RAY!
'RAY!
©1979 King Features Syndicate, Inc. World rights reserved.

NOW THE BAD NEWS... YOU'LL BE ROWING UPSTREAM
DIK BROWNE 3-17

A GLASS OF FRENCH MINERAL WATER, PLEASE
DIK BROWNE
5-30

AW, WHAT'S THAT GOT THAT OUR WATER DOESN'T ?
GAS
BURP!

AND GOOD MANNERS
EXCUSEZ-MOI

DO YOU KNOW WHAT TIME IT IS ?!!
DIK BROWNE
5-21
©1979 King Features Syndicate, Inc. World rights reserved.

WHERE ARE YOU GOING ?
THERE'S A CLOCK BACK AT THE CLUB

IT'S AN OLD TRICK—JUST BALANCE A CHAIR AGAINST THE DOOR
6-7

THEN, IF SOMEONE TRIES TO BREAK IN, YOU'LL HEAR THEM!
DIK BROWNE
©1979 King Features Syndicate, Inc. World rights reserved.

HAGAR
AM I LATE?
NO, WE'RE STILL DOING 'SHOW AND TELL'
I AM HAGAR THE HORRIBLE AND THIS IS MY MIGHTY SWORD 'SIGMUND' AND THIS IS MY MAGIC SHIELD 'GRETEL' AND THIS...
DIK BROWNE 3-11
© King Features Syndicate, Inc., 1974.

WHAT DID YOU BRING ME ?
SOMETHING FOR YOUR KITCHEN

OH, WOW! WHAT IS IT ?
A GARBAGE DISPOSAL
DIK BROWNE 6-14

BEAUTIFUL BABY!
©1979 King Features Syndicate, Inc. World rights reserved.

WAAH!

SMART, TOO!
DIK BROWNE 9-5

CAVIAR, SIRE, ?
HOW ELEGANT! YOU SURE HAVE COME UP IN THE WORLD...

DIK BROWNE 5-16
BUT YOU NEVER LOST THE ≈SIGH≈ COMMON TOUCH...

HAGAR, I CAN'T CLOSE THIS...
LET A VIKING DO IT!
© 1979 King Features Syndicate, Inc. World rights reserved.

WHUMP!

WHAT'S IN THIS THING ?
EGGS
4-13
DIK BROWNE

SWELL MEAL! HOW ABOUT DESSERT ?!
DIK BROWNE 7-6

SOON AS WE CLEAR THE TABLE

NO!
PLEASE!

NO PETS!

AND LET GO OF THAT EAGLE!
4-9
DIK BROWNE

ALL BEARS HIBERNATE IN WINTER
COULD SOME HAVE INSOMNIA ?

NO, THEY ALL SLEEP
IS IT POSSIBLE WINTER IS OVER ?
© King Features Syndicate, Inc., 1979. World rights reserved.

WHY ALL THESE DUMB QUESTIONS ?
1-31
DIK BROWNE

THIS IS WHERE I'M BUILDING MY DREAM CASTLE!
WHEN ARE YOU GOING TO START?
DIK BROWNE 1-27

START? WE'VE STARTED!
THUMP! THUMP!

I'VE GOT THE WINE CELLAR IN ALREADY

HAGAR! STOP PLAYING WITH YOUR FOOD!
DIK BROWNE 1-22

I'M ABOUT TO SERVE THE SPAGHETTI!

THERE IS SO MUCH IGNORANCE AND WAYWARDNESS I FEAR OUR WORK WILL NEVER END

TRUE, TRUE — BUT THE GREATER THE CHALLENGE— THE GREATER THE GLORY!

DIK BROWNE 1-23
THERE GOES A BIGGIE!

AND NOW A TOAST—
TO ONE WITHOUT WHOM
MY LIFE WOULD HAVE
BEEN INCOMPLETE...
© King Features Syndicate, Inc., 1979. World rights reserved.

ME!
1-25
DIK BROWNE

SVEN! I HEARD YOU GAVE UP BEING A VIKING...
YEAH, I DECIDED TO BECOME A MILLIONAIRE INSTEAD

SWELL! HOW ARE YOU DOING?

WELL, IT'S HARD GETTING STARTED...
GIVE
DIK BROWNE 2-1
© King Features Syndicate, Inc., 1979. World rights reserved.

ON TO VICTORY
ON TO VICTORY
VICTORY OR DEATH!!

WE HAVE 23 MEN
I THOUGHT WE HAD 22
DIK BROWNE 1-26

DID YOU COUNT NOSES LIKE I TOLD YOU?
THAT'S IT!

I MUST HAVE COUNTED YOU TWICE
© King Features Syndicate, Inc., 1979. World rights reserved.

WHAT DO YOU THINK, DR. ZOOK?
THAT'S A VERY SICK SHIP!

WORST CASE OF BARNACLES I'VE EVER SEEN!
2-2 DIK BROWNE

SOAKING YOUR FEET ?
THEY HURT
© King Features Syndicate, Inc., 1979. World rights reserved.

WHY DON'T YOU TAKE OFF YOUR SOCKS ?
EVEN MY SOCKS HURT
DIK BROWNE
1-30

YOU NEVER LISTEN TO A THING I SAY!!

NOT A THING! NOT A SINGLE THING!!

OH, NOT BAD... HOW WAS YOUR DAY?
5-28
DIK BROWNE

IT'S CALLED A LIFESAVER . IF A GUY CAN'T SWIM, YOU THROW IT TO HIM!

IS IT STRONG ?
DIK BROWNE
3-20
© King Features Syndicate, Inc., 1976. World rights reserved.

ARE YOU KIDDING? IT'S SOLID LEAD !
GOOD, GOOD
KLUNK!

CLEAN UP THIS SHIP! IT LOOKS LIKE A PIGPEN!
AYE, AYE

AND GET RID OF THAT GOAT, TOO!
OINK! OINK! OINK!
3-19
DIK BROWNE
© King Features Syndicate, Inc., 1976. World rights reserved.

THE TROUBLE WITH MEN IS — THEY'RE AFRAID OF WOMEN
© King Features Syndicate, Inc., 1976. World rights reserved.

DIK BROWNE
3-17
I WONDER WHY?

I'M NOT PUTTING WOMEN DOWN— I JUST SAY THEY'RE DIFFERENT!
© King Features Syndicate, Inc., 1976. World rights reserved.

WOW! WHOOPEE! HE FINALLY NOTICED!
3-18
DIK BROWNE

WHAT A VIKING! HE'LL TAKE ANYTHING THAT ISN'T NAILED DOWN!
© King Features Syndicate, Inc., 1976. World rights reserved.

QUICK! PULL THE NAILS FROM THAT BATH!
4-10 DIK BROWNE

HOW'S THE WEATHER OUT TODAY?

© King Features Syndicate, Inc., 1976. World rights reserved.

CHANGEABLE ..
4-9 DIK BROWNE

SIP! SLURP! SWISH!
GARGLE! GARGLE!
URK!
© King Features Syndicate, Inc., 1976. World rights reserved.
DIK BROWNE 4-7
SWISH! SWASH! SPLAT!

WHO ARE YOU?
I'M LOOKING FOR AN HONEST MAN

I'M AN HONEST MAN
REALLY?

WOULD I LIE TO YOU?
© King Features Syndicate, Inc., 1976. World rights reserved.
DIK BROWNE
3-13

DADDY TAUGHT ME A POEM TODAY
HAGAR TAUGHT YOU A POEM?! I CAN'T BELIEVE IT!

"OVER THE LIPS, PAST THE GUMS, LOOK OUT, STOMACH— HERE IT COMES!"

NOW I BELIEVE IT
DIK BROWNE
3-12
© King Features Syndicate, Inc., 1976. World rights reserved.

GET OFF THIS @☆!!#
FIELD, YOU ☆@*! BUM!

SHUT YOUR ☆!!*@#!
MOUTH, YOU !☆@! PIG!
4-8
DIK BROWNE

OKAY! SO MUCH FOR
DIPLOMACY!!

YOU CALL THIS SHARP? IT WOULDN'T CUT BUTTER!!
OH, YEAH? WATCH THIS!

SLASH!
GRUNT!
HACK!

© King Features Syndicate, Inc., 1976.
DIK BROWNE
3-10
BOY! THAT'S HARD BUTTER!

I WASN'T ABLE TO GET YOU A NEW DRESS SO I GOT YOU THIS
WHAT IS IT?
© King Features Syndicate, Inc., 1976. World rights reserved.

DIK BROWNE 3-9
RUST REMOVER

HIYA, SNERT...
HOW YOU
DOING?

THAT
GOOD,
EH?
© King Features Syndicate, Inc., 1976. World rights reserved.

I WISH PEOPLE HAD
TAILS SO WE COULD
TELL WHEN THEY'RE
REALLY HAPPY
DIK BROWNE
2-27

HURRY UP WITH THAT PICTURE! I DON'T HAVE ALL WEEK!!
© King Features Syndicate, Inc., 1976. World rights reserved.

THIS FISH IS BEGINNING TO SMELL!
2-26 DIK BROWNE

I AM HAGAR THE HORRIBLE—TERROR OF THE NORTH! SCOURGE OF EUROPE! LOOK UPON ME AND TREMBLE!
SOME TERROR!
YUK YUK!

KNOCK IT OFF, YOU GUYS, UNTIL I FINISH MY SPEECH!
2-24
DIK BROWNE
© King Features Syndicate, Inc., 1976.

WILL YOU CLEAR THE TABLE, DEAR?
SURE
© King Features Syndicate, Inc., 1976.

CRASH!
HEAVEN KNOWS HE TRIES
DIK BROWNE 2-25

HAGAR
GOT IT?
WHEN I RAISE MY HAND YOU WHACK IT WITH THE AX!

AWRIGHT, DUMMY!! THIS TIME I'M GOING TO NOD MY HEAD...
DIK BROWNE 2-23
© King Features Syndicate, Inc., 1976.

HAGAR
THIS @*!!% COUNTRY IS GETTING SOFT!
WE ARE NOT!!!

NOT **YOU**, STUPID! I SAID THIS COUNTRY IS GETTING SOFT!
© King Features Syndicate, Inc., 1977. World rights reserved.
3-28
DIK BROWNE

GASP!
YIIII
YOW
GASP!
WHAT'S WRONG WITH HONI?

SHE HAS TROUBLE GETTING INTO HER DRESS ON THESE COLD WINTER MORNINGS.
11-26
DIK BROWNE

C'MON, SNERT, ROLL OVER AND PLAY DEAD!

© King Features Syndicate, Inc., 1975. World rights reserved.

DIK BROWNE
11-28

OKAY— THAT'S CLOSE ENOUGH...

HAGAR
LET'S PULL A SNEAK RAID ON LONDON.
OKAY
11-24
DIK BROWNE

BUT FIRST WE'LL HAVE TO DISGUISE THE SHIP!

DO YOU THINK IT'LL WORK?
© King Features Syndicate, Inc., 1975. World rights reserved.

WANNA PLAY CHECKERS, DIRTY DIRK?
OKAY
© King Features Syndicate, Inc., 1975. World rights reserved.

BUT NO CHEATING!
ZOT!

I'LL BE DARNED! YOU WON THE FIRST GAME!
11-25 DIK BROWNE

THIS IS AN IMPORTED WINE...
© King Features Syndicate, Inc., 1975. World rights reserved.

WHERE IS IT IMPORTED FROM?

GLUG
GLUG

DIK BROWNE
11-27
TIBET

WHERE'S LUCKY EDDIE ?
I DON'T KNOW. I'VE LOOKED EVERYWHERE.

WELL, WE'LL JUST HAVE TO TEST THE NEW CATAPULT WITHOUT HIM...
zzZZZzz
DIK BROWNE 11-29
© King Features Syndicate, Inc., 1975. World rights reserved.

HAGAR
WHAT'S GOOD TO EAT?
EGGS
8-2
© King Features Syndicate, Inc., 1976. World rights reserved.

ARE THEY FRESH?

DIK BROWNE
ARE YOU KIDDING?

LUCKY EDDIE! LET GO THE ANCHOR!
AYE AYE
© King Features Syndicate, Inc., 1976.

SPLASH

LUCKY EDDIE! LET GO THE ANCHOR!
8-3
DIK BROWNE

MONEY! MONEY! MONEY!
ALL YOU GUYS WANT IS MONEY!!
WHAT DO YOU THINK I'M MADE OF?
© King Features Syndicate, Inc., 1976.
World rights reserved.
8-5
DIK BROWNE

IF WE GUESS, DO WE GET MONEY?

I TOLD YOU– THE WORLD IS FLAT!
WHAT ABOUT THIS?
DIK BROWNE
8-4

WHAT ABOUT IT?
BAM!
© King Features Syndicate, Inc., 1976.

I'LL BE DARNED! THE WORLD *IS* FLAT!

YOUR EYES ARE BLUE,
YOUR LIPS ARE, TOO...

MY LIPS
AREN'T BLUE

LISTEN, I'M A POET,
NOT A MAKEUP MAN
DIK BROWNE
8-6
© King Features Syndicate, Inc., 1976. World rights reserved.

AH-CHOO!
YOU SHOULD SEE A DOCTOR!

BAH! WHAT GOOD ARE DOCTORS ?!
© King Features Syndicate, Inc., 1976. World rights reserved.

THEY CAN CAST OUT DEMONS AND CHANGE BASE METALS TO GOLD, BUT THEY STILL CAN'T CURE THE COMMON COLD !!
DIK BROWNE
8-7

© King Features Syndicate, Inc., 1977.
World rights reserved.

-SIGH- DON'T TELL ME IT'S SPRING AGAIN!
3-29
DIK BROWNE

DON'T LIE TO ME! YOU KNOW CREAMED OYSTERS ARE A NO-NO!
I, ER...
© King Features Syndicate, Inc., 1977.

AND SO ARE PICKLED CHERRIES!
SHE'S SPOOKY!

HOW DID YOU KNOW?
MEN WITH BEARDS HAVE NO SECRETS
DIK BROWNE
3-30

SOMETIMES I WISH I WEREN'T A VIKING!
© King Features Syndicate, Inc., 1977.

IF YOU WEREN'T, YOU'D PROBABLY BE STUCK ON SOME CRUMMY FARM WITH A NAGGING WIFE, BAWLING KIDS, UP TO YOUR NECK IN DEBT —THEN WHERE WOULD YOU BE ?!!

HOME...
3-31
BROWNE

THIS IS THE "SINGING SWORD OF ANTIOCH"
REALLY?
DIK BROWNE
4-1

LISTEN...
COME TO ME MY MELANCHOLY BABY...
© King Features Syndicate, Inc., 1977. World rights reserved.

IT'S NOT THE EDGE OF THE WORLD! IT'S JUST A WATERFALL!
OH, GOOD!
4-2
DIK BROWNE

I THOUGHT WE WERE IN TROUBLE!

HAGAR
WILL THE HOUSE BE OKAY?
SURE, I TOLD LUCKY EDDIE TO WATER THE PLANTS AND LOCK UP THE LIQUOR...

EVEN HE CAN HANDLE THAT MUCH...
5-2
DIK BROWNE
© King Features Syndicate, Inc., 1977. World rights reserved.

SNEAKING IN AFTER MIDNIGHT, EH?
© King Features Syndicate, Inc., 1977. World rights reserved.

REMEMBER—IF YOU TELL A LIE YOUR HORNS WILL FALL OFF!
5-4
DIK BROWNE

WAIT FOR THE QUESTION! WAIT FOR THE QUESTION!!

© King Features Syndicate, Inc., 1977. World rights reserved.

BONK!

NAME DROPPER!!!
CORBINO
5-5 DIK BROWNE

I THOUGHT YOU LIKED THE LOOTING BUSINESS
I DO — BUT THE OVERHEAD IS KILLING ME —

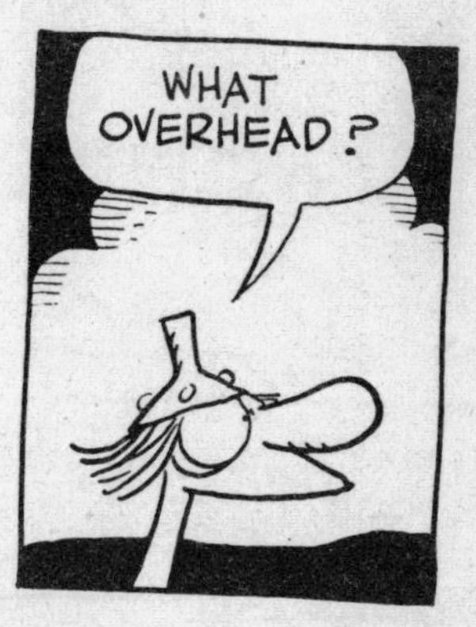
WHAT OVERHEAD ?

BONK!
OH...
5-6
DIK BROWNE
© King Features Syndicate, Inc., 1977.

I HEAR HAGAR BROUGHT YOU HOME A WORK OF ART...
BIG DEAL

LIKE EVERYTHING HE BRINGS HOME— IT'S BROKEN!
DIK BROWNE
5-7
© King Features Syndicate, Inc., 1977.

DIK BROWNE
12-1

VOOF!
© King Features Syndicate, Inc., 1976. World rights reserved.

SNERT... YOU'RE ONE LAZY DOG!

WHAT IS IT, DR. ZOOK?
WELL... YOU'VE HEARD OF SMALL POX?

NOW, HOLD STILL!
OKAY

BAM! BAM! BAM!
OKAY! ENOUGH! ENOUGH!

WELL, YOU'RE THE ONE WHO WANTED SWISS CHEESE!
DIK BROWNE
12-3

SHH! NOT A SOUND!
WHY?

THERE'S A BIG OLD MAN-EATING BEAR IN THERE, AND THE SLIGHTEST SOUND WOULD WARN HIM AND HE'D RUN AWAY.....
REALLY?

WAK!
AUK!
HOOT!
BOO!
DIK BROWNE
12-4

GET LUCKY EDDIE ... HE KNOWS HOW TO DO IT!
DIK BROWNE 3-12
© King Features Syndicate, Inc., 1974.

WHAT MAKES HIM SO SPECIAL ?

I USED TO BE A CHICKEN PLUCKER!

3·14

DIK BROWNE

© King Features Syndicate, Inc., 1974.

OKAY!—THANKS. YOU DON'T HAVE TO WATCH MY SEAT ANYMORE!

NOW REMEMBER, HAMLET—IT'S VERY IMPORTANT THAT YOU BRUSH YOUR TEETH AND ALWAYS WEAR CLEAN UNDERWEAR.
3-15

DAD, DO YOU ALWAYS WEAR CLEAN UNDERWEAR?

UNDERWEAR?
© King Features Syndicate, Inc., 1974.
DIK BROWNE

YOU KNOW THE TROUBLE WITH WOMEN?
© King Features Syndicate, Inc., 1974.

THEY DON'T KNOW HOW TO RELAX AND ENJOY LIFE.

AND THAT'S ANOTHER TROUBLE...THEY GOT ROTTEN TEMPERS!
DIK BROWNE
3-16

WILL YOU STICK A POKER IN THIS BEER?

PSSSSSS
© King Features Syndicate, Inc., 1976. World rights reserved.

I LIKE TO START THE DAY WITH A HOT BREAKFAST
5-11

YOU'RE SPOILING HIM— HE NEEDS DISCIPLINE
YOU DON'T WANT HIM TO GROW UP WILD
5-15
HE GETS HAIR ALL OVER THE FURNITURE
DIK BROWNE
THEY MUST BE TALKING ABOUT YOU, SNERT
© King Features Syndicate, Inc., 1976. World rights reserved.

WHAT'S THAT, DR. ZOOK?
I JUST INVENTED THE FIRST MECHANICAL DOG

I HAVEN'T GOT ALL THE BUGS OUT YET
DIK BROWNE 5-14

YOU SHOULD BE ASHAMED COMING HOME IN THAT CONDITION
5-12

WHAT ARE YOU YELPING ABOUT ?! I PUT MYSELF TO BED, DIDN'T I ?

DIK BROWNE
© King Features Syndicate, Inc., 1976. World rights reserved.

WHAT ARE YOU DUNKING IN YOUR BEER?

ANGEL FOOD CAKE
BOY! YOU **ARE** A BARBARIAN!
DIK BROWNE
3-19
© King Features Syndicate, Inc., 1974.

WHAT'S THE MATTER WITH YOUR FOOT?
IT'S ASLEEP
3-20

WHY IS IT DOING THAT?
I DON'T KNOW

DIK BROWNE
IT MUST BE DREAMING.
© King Features Syndicate, Inc., 1974.

HAGAR
IS IT JUST ME OR IS IT WARM IN HERE ?
DIK BROWNE .. 11-29
© King Features Syndicate, Inc., 1976. World rights reserved.

ALL I CAN DO IS GIVE YOU SOME TRANQUILIZERS

IS THAT THE BEST YOU CAN DO ?

SURE – REMEMBER, MODERN MEDICINE IS ONLY IN ITS INFANCY!
DIK BROWNE 3-23
© King Features Syndicate, Inc., 1974.

HAGAR
A VIKING SEWING?
'A STITCH IN TIME SAVES NINE!'
© King Features Syndicate, Inc., 1974.

YECH!
NO, REALLY!

DIK BROWNE
2-18
LOOK AT ALL THE STITCHES I'VE SAVED ALREADY.

THERE ARE ONLY TWO KINDS OF PEOPLE IN THIS WORLD — THE 'HAVES' AND 'HAVE-NOTS'!

WHICH ARE YOU?

I'M A 'GONNA GET'!
DIK BROWNE
2-19

DID DAD REALLY PUT LONDON TO THE TORCH?
THAT'S WHAT HE TELLS PEOPLE.
DIK BROWNE 2-21
© King Features Syndicate, Inc., 1974.

MUST HAVE BEEN BEGINNER'S LUCK.

YOU'RE GOING ON A DIET!
© King Features Syndicate, Inc., 1974.

DIK BROWNE
2-23
GRRRR!

YOU, TOO!

IF THAT'S FISH AGAIN, YOUR NAME IS MUD!! WHAT IS IT?!

DANISH PUDDING
BOY, ARE YOU LUCKY!
©King Features Syndicate, Inc., 1973.

OH... WATCH OUT FOR BONES
DIK BROWNE
12-11

SURE, I LOVE MY FAMILY— BUT A GUY'S GOT TO GET AWAY ONCE IN A WHILE TO RELAX...
DIK BROWNE 5-23

...AND ENJOY SOME ADULT CONVERSATION...
XXX

YOU HAVE A CASE OF 24-HOUR GALLOPING EAR WAX
WHAT?

I SAID YOU GOT EAR WAX
OH! IS IT CONTAGIOUS?
DIK BROWNE 5-22

WHAT?

"THE COW JUMPED OVER THE MOON..."

BOY! THAT WAS GREAT! WHAT KIND OF A STORY WAS THAT ?
©1979 King Features Syndicate, Inc. World rights reserved.

DIK BROWNE 6-1
SCIENCE FICTION

I'M GOING OUT TO RELAX A BIT, DEAR

BOY! TALK ABOUT DIRTY LOOKS!
6-4 DIK BROWNE
©1979 King Features Syndicate, Inc. World rights reserved.

SAY, ISN'T THAT 'SIR FORGETFUL' OVER THERE ?

YEP
6-16
DIK BROWNE
©1979 King Features Syndicate, Inc. World rights reserved.

WHAT ARE YOU DOING?
THROWING OUT THE VINEGAR. IT ALL WENT BAD.
CRACK!

THEY ALL TURNED TO WINE!
CRACK!
6-22
DIK BROWNE

WHY DID THE GODS MAKE MEN SO STUPID?
THERE MUST BE A REASON
DIK BROWNE

OF COURSE, IT DOES MAKE WOMEN LOOK GOOD!
THERE YOU ARE!
6-23

S'LONG, FELLOWS!
© 1979 King Features Syndicate Inc. World rights reserved

YOU BE CAREFUL! A PERSON IS JUDGED BY THE COMPANY HE KEEPS!

THAT'S OKAY. YOU'RE GOOD ENOUGH FOR ME.
DIK BROWNE 6-19

REMEMBER, BROTHER HAGAR—MODERATION!
YEAH... SURE
©1979 King Features Syndicate, Inc. World rights reserved.

IS MODERATION GOOD, HAGAR?
IF YOU DON'T OVERDO IT...
6-15
DIK BROWNE

HAGAR
WHICH ONE OF YOU GUYS ORDERED A DUCK-DOWN SUPER-FLUFFY KING-SIZE PILLOW?
© King Features Syndicate, Inc., 1979. World rights reserved.

GUESS!!
DIK BROWNE 1-15

I JUST SOLVED THE OIL SHORTAGE—
DIK BROWNE
7-11

I INVENTED A WAY TO GET TWICE AS MUCH OUT OF A BARREL!

TWO FAUCETS
©1979 King Features Syndicate, Inc. World rights reserved.

DON'T TRY TO TELL ME ABOUT MARRIAGE!

I WAS MARRIED BEFORE YOU WERE BORN!

YES, PAPA
6-8 DIK BROWNE

STOP SAYING THAT!

I KNOW YOU ARE SHY, LARS...
BUT YOU CAN'T EXPECT A GIRL TO MAKE THE FIRST MOVE

DIK BROWNE 7-5
OH... OKAY

WHAT ARE YOU DOING?
I'M CELEBRATING THE RITES OF SPRING

BUT IT ISN'T SPRING YET
1-31
DIK BROWNE
NEVER PUT OFF TILL TOMORROW WHAT YOU CAN DO TODAY

STOP THAT!
IT'S AN OLD CUSTOM TO THROW GLASSES AFTER A TOAST
CRASH!
TINKLE!
BROWNE-3-2

I DON'T CARE! PEOPLE WHO LIVE IN STONE HOUSES SHOULDN'T THROW GLASSES!
© King Features Syndicate, Inc., 1978.

HAGAR
WAIT'LL YOU HEAR WHAT HAPPENED TODAY!!

HOLD IT! REMEMBER NO BAD LANGUAGE OR VIOLENT TALK
© King Features Syndicate, Inc., 1978.

WELL, WHAT HAPPENED TODAY?
NOT MUCH
1-30
DIK BROWNE

MAMA! THERE'S A PRICE ON DADDY'S HEAD!
OH, THAT'S NOTHING!

IT'S JUST A NEW HAT...
DIK BROWNE
3-3
© King Features Syndicate, Inc., 1978. World rights reserved.

WHAT'S WRONG WITH HELGA?
AW, NOTHING
© King Features Syndicate, Inc., 1978.

SOMEONE TOLD HER, "THIS IS THE FIRST DAY OF THE REST OF YOUR LIFE."
2-24
BROWNE

I CAN'T TAKE MUCH MORE OF THIS!
COURAGE, HAGAR! THE BATTLE WILL SOON END!

WHO'S TALKING ABOUT BATTLES?!

IT'S THESE ROTTEN LUNCHES HELGA PACKS!
© King Features Syndicate, Inc., 1978.

WE HAVE ENOUGH FIREWOOD, HAGAR
CHOP!
CHOP!

NOW SHE TELLS ME!!
DIK BROWNE
3-25
© King Features Syndicate, Inc., 1978. World rights reserved.

IT IS SAID: "A man with a beard is never alone"
© King Features Syndicate, Inc., 1978.

OH... I SEE WHAT YOU MEAN...
DIK BROWNE
1-21
ITCH
ITCH

I CAN'T HEAR THE ENEMY
DON'T BE LAZY! PUT YOUR EAR TO THE GROUND!
© King Features Syndicate, Inc., 1978.

WELL, DO YOU HEAR ANYTHING?
DIK BROWNE 1-17

Z Z Z Z Z Z Z

THE SECRET OF MY SUCCESS IS SIMPLE — ALWAYS TRY TO MEET PEOPLE HALF WAY...

SOMETIMES EVEN MORE THAN HALF WAY

THAT'S CALLED A "SURPRISE ATTACK"
© King Features Syndicate, Inc., 1978.
DIK BROWNE
1-20

HEY! I JUST SAW LADY GODIVA ON HER HORSE!
SO WHAT!

THAT ACT IS OLD STUFF.
OH, YEAH?!

SHE GOT A HAIRCUT!
DIK BROWNE 1-10

HAGAR
WHAT A TERRIBLE NIGHT. YOU TOSSED AND TURNED ALL NIGHT
OH, DID IT BOTHER YOU ?
© King Features Syndicate, Inc., 1978. World rights reserved.

JUST THE TOSSING...
1-16
DIK BROWNE

HERE'S A FULL-BODIED CHEESE WITH A REAL PUNGENT AROMA

AW, DON'T TALK ABOUT IT! OPEN IT UP!
© King Features Syndicate, Inc., 1978.

WOW! THAT'S CHEESE!!
-- DIK BROWNE
1-12

PARDON ME, IS THIS 3203 NORTH ESSEX STREET?
YES, IT IS
© King Features Syndicate, Inc., 1978. World rights reserved.

THANK YOU.
THIS IS THE PLACE, MEN
1-11
DIK BROWNE

MOMMA! I GOT CAUGHT IN THE RAIN AND ALL THE CURL CAME OUT OF MY HAIR!

DON'T COMPLAIN!!
DIK BROWNE 1-14

MAKE SNERT STOP THAT!!
AW, ALL DOGS BURY BONES...
DIK BROWNE 4-1

I'M HERE TO COLLECT THE "HEAD TAX"
MORE NON-SENSE!

WHY IS IT CALLED THE "HEAD TAX" ANYWAY?
© King Features Syndicate, Inc.,

GUESS
DIK BROWNE 3-30

I HAVE A SUICIDE MISSION
WE'LL DRAW STRAWS TO SEE WHO GOES

LOOKS LIKE LUCKY EDDIE!
DIK BROWNE
3-22
© King Features Syndicate, Inc., 1978. World rights reserved.

HAGAR
LOOK! ANOTHER DAMSEL IN DISTRESS—THEY'RE AS BAD AS KNIGHTS IN SHINING ARMOR!
2-20
BROWNE

I THOUGHT YOU LIKED DAMSELS IN DISTRESS
© King Features Syndicate, Inc., 1978.

I DO— BUT THEY ATTRACT DRAGONS

HAGAR
WHAT SHAPE IS MY SHIP IN, MR. CARPENTER?
PRETTY GOOD
© King Features Syndicate, Inc., 1978.

IT JUST NEEDS A LITTLE DENTAL WORK
DIK BROWNE 3-20

ARE WE LIVING IN THE MIDDLE AGES OR THE DARK AGES?
© King Features Syndicate, Inc.,

DARK AGES
3-29
DIK BROWNE

IT'S CALLED "THE WINE OF FORGETFULNESS"
GOOD, VERY GOOD

HEY, YOU FORGOT TO PAY!
FOR WHAT?

GEE! I HOPE THIS BRAND DOESN'T CATCH ON!
© King Features Syndicate, Inc.,
DIK BROWNE 3-31

WHAT DO I DO THAT'S SO WRONG? JUST TELL ME!!

FIRST...
I SHOULD HAVE KNOWN SHE'D HAVE A LIST!
DIK BROWNE
3-28

IT'S THE ROYAL CENSUS. HOW OLD ARE YOU, MRS. HAGAR?
FORTY

...ISH
© King Features Syndicate, Inc., 1978.
3-21 DIK BROWNE

KIDS TODAY ARE SPOILED!! LET ME TELL YOU WHAT IT WAS LIKE WHEN I WAS YOUNG!

2-28
DIK BROWNE

IT'S CALLED A COCONUT AND IT'S FULL OF MILK
© King Features Syndicate, Inc., 1978. World rights reserved.

HOW DO YOU GET IT OUT ?
LISTEN
2-21

YOU JUST GOTTA SQUEEZE REAL HARD

HOLD IT, LUCKY EDDIE! LET ME TELL WHAT HAPPENED

YOU GET EVERYTHING BACKWARDS!
I DO NOT!
3-1
BROWNE

REMEMBER...
WHEN YOU MEET SOMEONE,
ALWAYS LOOK HIM RIGHT IN
THE EYE AND
SMILE...
DIK BROWNE
2-18

THEN GIVE HIM
A WARM, FIRM
HANDSHAKE!
© King Features Syndicate, Inc., 1978. World rights reserved.

THAT WAY HE CAN'T
GET AT HIS SWORD

YOU DON'T HAVE TO STARVE TO LOSE WEIGHT
JUST EAT HALF OF THE PORTIONS OF EACH COURSE

A NEW POT? HOW NICE!
© King Features Syndicate, Inc., 1978. World rights reserved.
2-7
DIK BROWNE

DIK BROWNE 2-9
© King Features Syndicate, Inc., 1978.
OH, WELL... HELP ME WIND HIM UP AGAIN.

WELL, HE DOES WORK HARD AND A MAN HAS TO UNWIND SOMETIMES...
I SUPPOSE SO...

YOU CAN'T DO ANYTHING RIGHT!!!

YOU CAN'T EVEN SHARPEN A BLADE PROPERLY!!

IT FEELS SHARP TO ME
IT SHOULD BE. IT USED TO BE A 6-FOOT SWORD!
© King Features Syndicate, Inc., 1978.
DIK
2-8

THE WORLD IS FLAT...
ONE MINUTE...

BAM! BAM!
© King Features Syndicate, Inc., 1978. World rights reserved.

NOW IT IS!
DIK BROWNE 2-16

OH! WHO LEFT THAT DOOR OPEN AGAIN?!!
5-3
© King Features Syndicate, Inc., 1977. World rights reserved.

DO ANIMALS KNOW WHAT YOU'RE THINKING?

SNERT DOES!
DIK BROWNE - 8-23

HAGAR
YOU LOOK BEAT! WHAT DID YOU DO TODAY?
SCRUBBED THE STEPS

IS THAT ALL?

THIS IS OUR FAMOUS PUFF PASTRY
WOW!
© King Features Syndicate, Inc., 1978. World rights reserved.

WHY DO THEY CALL IT 'PUFF PASTRY'?

OH...
PUFF
DIK BROWNE 8-10

HAGAR... WHAT IS AN ISLAND?
© King Features Syndicate, Inc., 1978.

AN ISLAND IS A BODY OF LAND SURROUNDED BY WATER... ANY OTHER QUESTIONS?

YEAH... DOES AN ISLAND HAVE EYES?
DIK BROWNE
4-26

© King Features Syndicate, Inc., 1978. World rights reserved.

I'VE HAD THIS TUNE RUNNING THROUGH MY HEAD
4-19
DIK BROWNE

WHAT'S THAT ?

YEAH, I'M THE NEW KING OF IRELAND!
HOW DID YOU DO THAT?

I OWE IT ALL TO THE LITTLE PEOPLE WHO MADE IT POSSIBLE!

TELL IT, BROTHER !!
RIGHT ON!
4-5
DIK BROWNE
© King Features Syndicate, Inc., 1978.

HAGAR
HOLD STILL AND STOP COMPLAINING!
I CAN'T HELP IT!

I *HATE* HAIRCUTS!
© King Features Syndicate, Inc., 1978. World rights reserved.
DIK BROWNE
8-14

HAGAR
WEREN'T YOU THE EVIL KING'S JESTER ?
YES, I USED TO DO POLITICAL SATIRE

WHAT ARE YOU DOING NOW ?

20 YEARS
© King Features Syndicate, Inc., 1978.
DIK BROWNE - 8-7

BOY! DOES THAT FEEL GOOD!

DON'T LOOK AT ME LIKE THAT! MY FEET HURT! WHAT DO YOU WANT FROM ME ?!!

GET YOUR FEET OUTTA MY SOUP!
DIK BROWNE 8-15
© King Features Syndicate, Inc., 1978.

"THE SEA OF NO-RETURN"! HOW WILL WE FIND OUR WAY BACK?
I THOUGHT OF THAT

LUCKY EDDIE IS LEAVING A TRAIL OF BREAD CRUMBS
8-8 DIK BROWNE
© King Features Syndicate, Inc., 1978. World rights reserved.

WHAT KIND OF FISH ARE THOSE?
DIK BROWNE
7-11

FLYING FISH
© King Features Syndicate, Inc., 1978.

SORRY I'M LATE, HELGA

WHAT'S FOR DINNER ?
BROWNE 1-18

THIS IS LUCKY EDDIE, MY RIGHT-HAND MAN
© King Features Syndicate, Inc., 1978.
2-22
DIK BROWNE

THAT'S YOUR LEFT HAND, STUPID!

HEAR ANYTHING ?
HORSES
STANDING STILL
DIK BROWNE — 1-18
© King Features Syndicate, Inc., 1979. World rights reserved.

HOW CAN YOU TELL IF THEY'RE STANDING STILL ?
THEY'RE ARGUING

HOW MUCH FOR A PAIR OF SCISSORS?
THIS PAIR? 10 DRACMAS
DIK BROWNE 1-19

OH...ER... WELL, LET ME HAVE ONE SCISS

HOW ABOUT A BATHROBE FOR MR. HAGAR?

HOW MUCH?
TEN KRONER
© King Features Syndicate, Inc., 1979. World rights reserved.

TOO MUCH TO SPEND ON ONE BATH A YEAR
1-20
DIK BROWNE

HAGAR! I'M GETTING DIZZY!
9-3
© 1979 King Features Syndicate, Inc. World rights reserved.

I TOLD YOU: "DON'T LOOK DOWN!"
DIK BROWNE

AND SO, IN CONCLUSION...

I FEEL I CAN SAY THIS WITHOUT FEAR OF CONTRADICTION...
1-3 DIK BROWNE

DID YOU WANT YOUR EGG HARD OR SOFT-BOILED ?
HARD

OH, GOOD
DIK BROWNE - 1-4
© King Features Syndicate, Inc., 1978. World rights reserved.

HAGAR
IT'S AMAZING HOW DADDY CAN GET UP EARLY AND GO TO WORK AFTER A LATE NIGHT ON THE TOWN
YES, I DON'T KNOW HOW HE DOES IT!

Z Z Z Z
© King Features Syndicate, Inc., 1978. World rights reserved.
1-1
DIK BROWNE

I CAN'T DECIDE WHETHER TO MARRY OR BECOME A VIKING WARRIOR-MAIDEN
© King Features Syndicate, Inc., 1978. World rights reserved.

WHAT SHOULD I DO, MAMA?
WHY DON'T YOU SET THE TABLE ?
DIK BROWNE 1-6

I'LL FIND OUT WHERE ALL THE LIQUOR IS GOING!
I'LL MARK IT!
DIK BROWNE 2-13

GOOD IDEA!

QUICK! SET THE TABLE! REMEMBER — KNIVES ON THE RIGHT!
OKAY

NOW WHAT?
2-15 DIK BROWNE
© King Features Syndicate, Inc., 1979. World rights reserved.

LUCKY EDDIE! DON'T LET THE ENEMY SEE YOU'RE AFRAID!

GULP
I'LL TRY...
DIK BROWNE

OKAY... I'M READY
DIK BROWNE
1-5

© King Features Syndicate, Inc., 1979. World rights reserved.

NOPE! NO FISH HERE EITHER!
2-14
DIK BROWNE

ANYTHING GOOD LEFT ?
FIRE SALE
SURE
8-17

DIK BROWNE
F
HERE'S A BEAUT !

I MISS MY OLD BEDROOM. I HAVEN'T BEEN ABLE TO SLEEP FOR A WEEK!
HOW ABOUT HAGAR?
8-18

OH, YOU KNOW HAGAR— HE CAN SLEEP ANYWHERE
ZZZZZ
DIK BROWNE

IT MUST BE HARD TO FIGHT WITH HAGAR
NOT REALLY

THE HARD PART IS GETTING HIS ATTENTION
DIK BROWNE 8-23
PLINK

I'LL BET YOU CAN'T TOUCH YOUR NOSE WITH YOUR TONGUE!
I'LL BET I CAN!
HEY! THAT'S HARD!

GEE... THESE GUYS HAVE BEEN AT SEA TOO LONG!
UNHH!
RRR
UM!
DIK BROWNE 8-24

YUCK! HOW CAN YOU DRINK THAT HORRIBLE, SMELLY, UGLY STUFF ?!
XXX

WILL POWER
XXX
DIK BROWNE 8-25

LUCKY EDDIE IS A NICKNAME — MY REAL NAME IS TOO HARD TO PRONOUNCE
WHAT IS IT?

ÈÅØX̮ÜÇÑẐṔ
8-16

WOW!
DIK BROWNE

THIS YOUR FIRST RAID ?
YEAH... TELL ME ARE THE ENGLISH TOUGH ?
ENGLAND

LET ME PUT IT THIS WAY...THEY LIVE HERE
TOUGH!
2-7

WORST STAINS I EVER SAW!
DID YOU GET THEM OUT?
8-15

FINALLY...
DIK BROWNE

YOUR HOVEL TAX IS DUE!!

THIS IS RIDICULOUS! NEXT YOU'LL BE TAXING THE AIR WE BREATHE!
8-14
DIK BROWNE

AIR?

HAGAR, DO YOU WANT ROAST BEEF TONIGHT?
8-9
DIK BROWNE

BZZZ
BZZ
BZZ

MAYBE
I HATE IT WHEN HE BRINGS HIS LAWYER HOME FOR DINNER
©1979 King Features Syndicate, Inc. World rights reserved.

18 IS TOO YOUNG TO GET MARRIED.

YOU KNOW NOTHING OF LIFE, LOVE, PAIN POWER, PASSION —THE WORLD!

WAIT A YEAR!

IT SOUNDS LIKE THIS WILL BE **SOME** YEAR!
DIK BROWNE 8-10

MY FOOT IS ASLEEP
WELL, JUST SHAKE IT.

NAW... IT PROBABLY NEEDS THE REST.
DIK BROWNE - 8-8

C'MON! LET'S GO!
I'M SO HUNGRY I COULD EAT A HORSE!

NOW WHERE DID BUTTERCUP GO TO?
DIK BROWNE
8-11
©1979 King Features Syndicate, Inc. World rights reserved.

NOTICE THAT I'M WEARING A NEW PERFUME?
OF COURSE

LOOKS GOOD.
DIK BROWNE
2-6

BOY! I'VE NEVER SEEN IT FAIL!

I ALWAYS GET STUCK IN THE SLOW LINE!

DOPE! VIKINGS DON'T BLOW BUBBLES!

GULP!
USE YOUR HEAD!

DIK BROWNE 2-10
© King Features Syndicate, Inc., 1979. World rights reserved.

DON'T WALK ON MY CLEAN FLOOR WITH YOUR DIRTY FEET!

AND NEXT TIME WASH YOUR HANDS!
2·5 DIK BROWNE

BET YOU KIDS NEVER SAW A REAL VIKING BEFORE!
©1979 King Features Syndicate, Inc. World rights reserved.

IST DAS EINE MOO?
JA, UND MILCH

BEAT IT! YOU DUMB KIDS!
MAMA!! EINE MADDEN MOO COW!
8-6
DIK BROWNE

THIS IS THE MOMENT OF DECISION!

ARE YOU HEROES OR CRAVEN COWARDS?
8-7
DIK BROWNE

10 HEROES... 10 CRAVEN COWARDS AND 2 UNDECIDED

I GIVE UP! I JUST CAN'T MAKE THIN PANCAKES!
POUND!
POUND!

OH, WELL, I'LL DO SOMETHING ELSE...
© 1979 King Features Syndicate, Inc. World rights reserved.

DIK BROWNE 7-14
I'LL MAKE A POUND CAKE
POUND
POUND
POUND

THE WORLD IS FLAT!
YOU WANNA KNOW SOMETHING ELSE?

IT'S ALSO CROOKED!
DIK BROWNE 9-14
© King Features Syndicate, Inc., 1977.

I'M JUST GOING OUT TO SACK STUTTGART
DON'T GIVE ME THAT!

YOU'RE WEARING YOUR NEW COAT... FANCY SHIELD... LILAC WATER...
3-12

YOU'RE GOING TO PILLAGE PARIS!
ONLY IF THE WEATHER IS NICE
DIK BROWNE

YOU GOT A NICE HOUSE... A LOVELY FAMILY...
DIK BROWNE 3-14

WHAT MORE COULD YOU ASK FOR?

BOY! THERE'S ALWAYS SOMETHING!
©1979 King Features Syndicate, Inc. World rights reserved.

I'M SORRY—BUT GARDENING IS WOMEN'S WORK

YOU MIGHT AT LEAST HELP WITH THE WEEDING!
9-4
DIK BROWNE
©1979 King Features Syndicate, Inc. World rights reserved.

DAD, IF YOU WEREN'T A VIKING, WHAT WOULD YOU BE ?

DIK BROWNE
1-17

SAD...

THAT WATER LOOKS DIRTY!
OH, STOP COMPLAINING
6-6 DIK BROWNE-

OW!!

I FOUND THE MISSING FORK, HONI!

MEN! I WANT YOU TO ROW LIKE YOU NEVER ROWED BEFORE!

EVERYBODY'S A COMEDIAN...
DIK BROWNE 2-16
© King Features Syndicate, Inc., 1979. World rights reserved.

Z
Z
©1979 King Features Syndicate, Inc. World rights reserved.

AGHHHH!!!

WIVES WITH COLD FEET SHOULD BE ILLEGAL!
6-26 DIK BROWNE

WHAT A DROOPY PLANT!
WHAT DO YOU KNOW? SHE'LL LOVE IT!

IT'S PERFECT!
DIK BROWNE 6-25

THERE'S ONLY ONE THING I'M ABSOLUTELY SURE OF IN THIS WORLD!

THE WORLD IS FLAT!
©1979 King Features Syndicate, Inc. World rights reserved.

I THINK
6-30
DIK BROWNE

THIS IS A FULL-BODIED WINE

DIK BROWNE
8-22

PLOP!
I'LL SAY

LUCKY EDDIE, YOU SHOULD BE MORE SERIOUS ABOUT YOUR FUTURE

YOU OUGHT TO GET MARRIED

THAT'D WIPE THAT SILLY GRIN OFF YOUR FACE.
DIK BROWNE
8-21

I HATE TO HAVE YOU GIVE UP YOUR BEDROOM EVERY TIME I VISIT YOU
NONSENSE, MOTHER. WE DON'T MIND, DO WE, HAGAR ?
8-20
DIK BROWNE

I SAID-WE DON'T MIND, DO WE, HAGAR ?

IS THAT WATER FRESH ?
PRACTICALLY.

?
DIK BROWNE
7-26

DID YOU OPEN HAMLET'S PRESENT TO YOU ?
NO, NOT YET

I HOPE IT'S NOT ANOTHER FROG
7-27 DIK BROWNE
©1979 King Features Syndicate, Inc. World rights reserved.

WE SURRENDER
THE CASTLE IS MINE!
NOT QUITE!
7-21

TITLE SEARCH
CLOSING COSTS
LEGAL FEES
DIK BROWNE
©1979 King Features Syndicate, Inc. World rights reserved.

?
WHAT'S UNDER THERE?
?
6-28
DIK BROWNE

UNDER WHERE?
THAT'S WHAT I THOUGHT

?

BEFORE I MET HAGAR I ALMOST MARRIED THE KING OF FRANCE
REALLY? WHICH ONE?

CHARLES THE FORTUNATE
DIK BROWNE 6-29

HIC!
THIS'LL CURE IT! BREATHE INTO THIS BAG...

FFFFFFFFF
DIK 7-7 BROWNE

BAM!
HIC HIC HIC
HIC HIC HIC
HIC
HIC
HIC HIC
HIC
HIC
HIC
HIC
HIC
HIC

I HOPE YOU GROW UP TO BE HALF THE MAN YOUR FATHER IS!
DIK BROWNE
7-4
©1979 King Features Syndicate, Inc. World rights reserved.

OF COURSE, YOU'LL HAVE TO WATCH YOUR DIET

©1979 King Features Syndicate, Inc. World rights reserved.

DIK BROWNE
7-2

DAD! I CAUGHT A FIREFLY!
LET ME SEE!

7-13

MY! THAT'S A BIG ONE!
DIK BROWNE

HEADS WE INVADE SUNNY ITALY — TAILS IT'S ENGLAND
8-4
DIK BROWNE

THEY OUGHTA OUTLAW GAMBLING!
LONDON
©1979 King Features Syndicate, Inc. World rights reserved.

DRINK...DRINK...DRINK...
DRINK...DRINK...DRINK...
DRINK...DRINK...DRINK...
DRINK...DRINK...DRINK...

©1979 King Features Syndicate, Inc. World rights reserved.
DIK BROWNE
8-27

BOY! YOU CAN'T BEAT THOSE OLD VIKING DRINKING SONGS!

DIK BROWNE
8-28

SHWERP!
© 1979 King Features Syndicate, Inc.

WHERE'S DINNER ?
IT HAS TO COOK SOME MORE

A TABLE FOR TWO
YES, SIR

HOW DID WE GET SUCH A GREAT TABLE ?
BECAUSE... "MONEY TALKS"
8-29
DIK BROWNE

?

DIK BROWNE
8-30

?

TELLING HIM ABOUT NATURE?
TAXES

HONI! DON'T YOU KNOW THAT "A WATCHED KETTLE DOESN'T BOIL"?

I DON'T BELIEVE IT!

IT'S JUST A SAYING
DIK BROWNE 8-31
©1979 King Features Syndicate, Inc. World rights reserved.

HURRY, HONI, BEFORE THE SIEGE ENDS!
DIK BROWNE 9-1

IT'S A WONDERFUL CHANCE TO CLEAN OUT THE ATTIC!!

NOW WATCH YOUR MANNERS. THE HANSENS ARE ONE OF THE OLDEST FAMILIES IN NORWAY!
©1979 King Features Syndicate, Inc. World rights reserved.

WILL YOU GET THE DOOR, JUNIOR?
OKAY, DAD
DIK BROWNE
8-1

WHAT ARE YOU DOING?
PRACTICING CHECKERS

WITH ONLY ONE CHECKER?
I'M JUST PRACTICING JUMPING
DIK BROWNE 8-3

HOLD IT THERE! DON'T COME IN!
8-2
DIK BROWNE

FIRST I WANT TO SEE YOU WALK A STRAIGHT LINE

NOT YOU! HIM!

WHY DON'T WE EVER TALK ANYMORE?
CHOMP! CHOMP! CHOMP!

MMBFGLM...SMACK... FFLUGMMBM...GLOMB... MMMWEEBM...CHOMP...

FORGET IT
CHOMP! CHOMP! CHOMP...
DIK BROWNE 7-30
Syndicate, Inc. World rights reserved.

WHAT DOES IT LOOK LIKE I'M DOING ?! I'M PACKING A LUNCH !
DIK BROWNE 6-12

TO GO TO *BED* ?
©1979 King Features Syndicate, Inc. World rights reserved.

GENTLY! GENTLY! CHABLIS IS AN EXCELLENT WINE BUT IT TRAVELS POORLY!
WHERE'S THE WINE?
XXX

IN HIM.
XXX
DIK BROWNE
5-18
©1979 King Features Syndicate, Inc. World rights reserved.

FAREWELL!
I GO TO FIND FAME AS AN EXPLORER!

©1979 King Features Syndicate, Inc. World rights reserved.
SLAM!

HAMLET, LET YOUR FATHER OUT OF THE CLOSET
5-19 DIK BROWNE

YAWN
BOY... WHAT A DREAM!
DIK BROWNE 5-14

...ER... WAS I TALKING IN MY SLEEP AGAIN?

LOOKING AT THE STARS SURE MAKES YOU THINK, DOESN'T IT, DAD?
YEAH, IT DOES

THEY'RE SO LITTLE AND PUNY AND WE'RE SO BIG!
DIK BROWNE 5-15

KEEP ALERT! WE MUST BE NEAR ESKIMO LAND!

ARE IGLOOS EVER POINTY ON TOP?
OF COURSE NOT! WHY?

JUST ASKING
DIK BROWNE - 7-28

HOW CAN WE TEACH SNERT NOT TO BEG FOR FOOD AT THE TABLE ?
VOOF!
7-24

LET HIM TRY A FEW BITES
DIK BROWNE
©1979 King Features Syndicate, Inc. World rights reserved.

DO YOU WANT A DRINK?
MAYBE

DON'T BE SO WISHY-WASHY! TALK UP LIKE A VIKING!! BE POSITIVE!

NOW- DO YOU WANT A DRINK?
DIK BROWNE 7-23

MAYBE!!

DADDY, THIS IS MY NEW BOYFRIEND 'AXEL THE BOLD'

AXEL THE BOLD? THAT'S MORE LIKE IT!
BAM!

OH, NOW YOU FRIGHTENED HIM!
7-18
DIK BROWNE

THE TURKS!
DON'T WORRY, WE'LL BE ALL RIGHT...
7-17 DIK BROWNE

...IF WE DON'T LOSE OUR HEADS!

IT'S JUST AN EXPRESSION!

YOU KNOW, SNERT, YOU'RE PRACTICALLY HUMAN!

OW!

I MEANT THAT AS A COMPLIMENT
DIK BROWNE - 7-16

PUT A LIGHT IN THE WINDOW–I'LL BE BACK IN A TRICE!

IS A TRICE A LONG TIME, MAMA?
7-20
DIK BROWNE

IT IS, IF I KNOW YOUR FATHER
© 1979 King Features Syndicate, Inc. World rights reserved.

WHAT A NIGHT!
I'M SO STIFF I CAN'T EVEN STRAIGHTEN UP...
7-19
DIK BROWNE

MUST'A SLEPT IN A DRAFT!

I DIDN'T EXPECT HAGAR TO BE HOME
WHY, AUNT NUDGE, HE LOOKS FORWARD TO YOUR VISITS.

DON'T YOU, DEAR?
©1979 King Features Syndicate, Inc. World rights reserved.
7-9
DIK BROWNE

VENICE IS MY KIND OF TOWN!
WHAT ARE THOSE?
© 1979 King Features Syndicate, Inc. World rights reserved.

PEDESTRIANS
DIK BROWNE 9-6

BOY! I WISH I WERE YOUR AGE AND KNEW EVERYTHING I KNOW TODAY!
©1979 King Features Syndicate, Inc. World rights reserved.

YOU STILL WOULDN'T KNOW HOW TO TIE YOUR SHOELACES!
DIK BROWNE 9-8

IF YOU'RE GOING TO HAVE ONE YOU'VE GOT TO TRAIN HIM! SHOW HIM YOU'RE THE MASTER!

BUT ISN'T THAT PUPPY TOO YOUNG FOR THAT?

DIK BROWNE
10-31
I'M TALKING ABOUT MEN—
BUTT OUT!!
©King Features Syndicate, Inc., 1973.

MY MOTHER IS GOING TO VISIT US!
NO, SHE AIN'T!
YES, SHE IS! YES!
NO, SHE'S NOT!

WAIT, THIS IS SILLY... WHY DON'T WE SETTLE THIS LIKE ADULTS?
OKAY

BEST TWO OUT OF THREE, OKAY?
DIK BROWNE 10-3
©King Features Syndicate, Inc., 1973.

YOU SPENT ALL MY MONEY ?!!
DON'T SHOUT!
© King Features Syndicate, Inc., 1978. World rights reserved.

DO YOU WANT THE WHOLE WORLD TO KNOW OUR BUSINESS ?!
IK BROWNE 7-19

HAGAR
© King Features Syndicate, Inc., 1978.
I FORGOT MY KEY
WHAT'LL YOU DO ?

SOMETIMES HELGA LEAVES ONE UNDER THE DRAWBRIDGE
4-10
DIK BROWNE

IT'S LATE—I HOPE WE'RE NOT KEEPING YOU FOLKS UP
CERTAINLY NOT! CAN I GET YOU SOMETHING ELSE?

HOW ABOUT BREAKFAST?
9-15.
DIK BROWNE

HELGA! I'VE FINISHED BEATING YOUR RUG!
© King Features Syndicate, Inc., 1978.

SIGH
HE TRIES, GOODNESS KNOWS...
11-11 DIK BROWNE

WHY ISN'T HE PLAYING?
HAS HE LOST HIS LIP?
NO... HE JUST CAN'T FIND IT!

REMEMBER — A VIKING FIGHTS HARD, BUT—

A VIKING FIGHTS CLEAN!
I THINK HE'S HINTING, DIRTY DIRK

I CAN'T OPEN THIS BOTTLE OF CHAMPAGNE
SURE YOU CAN... JUST KEEP TRYING

POP!

LET GO OF THE CORK!!!
10-31
DIK BROWNE
© King Features Syndicate, Inc., 1978.

HAGAR
HOW CAN YOU STAND BARE LEGS IN THIS COLD?
BECAUSE— WE'RE SCOTS!

HOW ABOUT THAT GUY?

OH... THAT'S A SCOT WITH POOR CIRCULATION
2-6 DIK BROWNE

I GOTTA BACK-ACHE
YOU SHOULD DRINK SAUERKRAUT JUICE LIKE MY FATHER ALWAYS DID

YOUR FATHER WAS **FULL** OF ACHES AND PAINS!
THAT'S ALL RIGHT, HE STILL DRANK SAUERKRAUT JUICE EVERY DAY!
DIK BROWNE
1-24

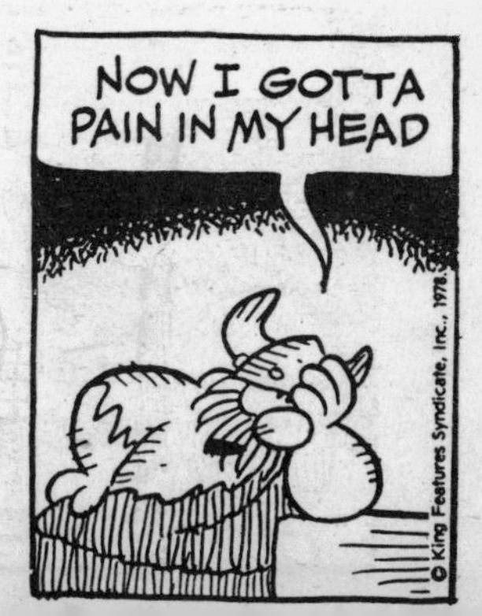
NOW I GOTTA PAIN IN MY HEAD
© King Features Syndicate, Inc., 1978.

NOW WE TAKE THE VIKING OATH- 'VICTORY OR DEATH' -RAISE YOUR RIGHT HANDS!
DIK BROWNE 8-26

YOU TOO!